BUNDLA JOY
THE CHRISTMAS STORY

Christopher,
Best Wishes
And Dreams Come
True!

Christmas 1987

Written by:
Stephen Cosgrove
and

Illustrated by:
Louise Zingerelli

Rainforest
PUBLISHING

Library Of Congress Cataloging in Publication Data
Cosgrove, Stephen
Bundla Joy: The Christmas Story
Bundla Joy, a young bear, and Piffany, a winged deer, set out to rescue the Morning Star and Piffany's mother from the icy clutches of the monstrous dragon Evilspell. *****

Dedicated to the spirit of Christmas past and my treasured wife, Shaerie, who came and shared the dreams of the DreamMaker.

Stephen

There was a place, a wondrous place, beyond your imagination. A place with graceful mountain valleys and high jagged peaks. A place created by the ices of ages long ago and protected from the eyes of older men by their lack of hopes and dreams. They called this place Kapriol.

Kapriol was made not only of dreams, but of forests of gigantic pine and scented cedar. It was a land of rich loamy soil and colorful, sweet-smelling blossoms in the spring. Each fall, Kapriol's forest rang with the deep honking of rare arctic geese as they prepared to fly back to winter's reality. Kapriol was many things. . .forests, mountains, and nature's seasons.

One such year, just days before Christmas Eve, a strange, winged deer named Piffany flew silhouetted against the bitterly cold night sky. Her wings were of white gossamer down and her coat was like the silvered fur of a new-born fawn in spring.

Soaring above the forest, she circled the purpled skies, searching for somewhere to light and rest. She widened her pattern until she suddenly sighted beneath her a quaint, little village nestled in the woods.

Carefully, she spiraled around and around, lighting down in the courtyard of the quiet little town. Her tiny feet clicked loudly on the cobblestone street and echoed throughout the empty alleys. She looked about, but nothing stirred.

This creature of flight clicked her way through all the empty streets and by ways that made up the village. She stopped here and there to gaze in the window or doorway of a charming cottage. All she found was waiting and wanting. No living thing stirred and the air was softly still.

She rounded a shop corner and suddenly stopped. Her mouth opened in shock, for there before her were bears — all sorts of bears — asleep in the most peculiar fashion! There were brown bears, honey bears, black bears, and all of them seemed to have fallen asleep as they sat about a large, unlit Christmas tree in the courtyard of the village. Like a daisy chain, they held each others' large, furry paws. From the babies to the aged ones, they lay in peaceful, blissful sleep.

"That's a bit queer!" Piffany said in her soft, velvet voice. "I know bears sleep throughout the winter, but they always stay awake until the day after Christmas. Not a day before and not two days after." She walked daintily around the tree and looked at each bear. They all remained asleep, snoring soundly.

Piffany's hooves clicked on the cobblestones as she walked round and round the tree. She stopped and gently nudged one of the bears with a slender foreleg and said, "Mr. Bear, oh, Mr. Bear. I wish to know why all of you are sleeping before Christmas and not the day after?" But no matter how she prodded and poked, and no matter what question she asked, the bears would not wake.

"Mr. Bear, oh, Mr. Bear. I wish to know why
all of you are sleeping..."

She stepped back and looked at the square, the sleeping bears, the presents unopened, and the dark Christmas tree. "Oh, the Christmas tree!" For the first time she noticed that the very top of the tree was bare. "That's a bit odd!" she said as she walked around the tree. "There's always a star on Christmas trees!"

She was startled out of her reverie by a soft, snuffling noise. She whirled toward the sound, but saw nothing there. Piffany stopped, cocked her ears, and listened closely. Once again the snuffling came. But this time she heard exactly where it had come from: the alley at the edge of the courtyard.

Nostrils flared and huge wings spread for instant flight, Piffany slowly stepped to the edge of the alley toward the mysterious sound. The noise of hooves touching on stone seemed to echo throughout the night. Slowly, she peered around the corner and saw — nothing.

As she turned away, a cast-off pile of furs heaped against the wall gave another loud, "Shhlurrff!" Piffany nearly fell over herself as she snapped her head back around the corner. She was so frightened that her legs slipped out from under her and she fell — a heap of white wings and long, gangly legs.

Piffany was ready to fly away, so afraid was she. She unfurled her wings and was just ready to cast herself into the sky when the frightening snuffling became the sound of someone crying. She paused for a moment or two and listened very carefully. Sure enough, she hadn't been hearing the sounds of some wild beast, but rather the chokes and sobs of a frightened creature.

"Who are you?" Piffany asked in a gentle voice. "Who are you and why do you cry?"

The pile of fur rolled about until two large, brown eyes looked up at Piffany. "My name is Bundla Joy." Quickly the little creature regained his self-confidence and asked, "Who are you?"

"My name is Piffany. I have flown to your land in search of my mother, who disappeared from our ancestral herd. I landed in your village because I was tired and needed rest and water."

Suddenly, as if reminded of something, Bundla jumped to his chubby little feet and waddled down the alley to the courtyard of the Christmas tree. Piffany followed cautiously behind. The little cub ran round the tree until he found an older, female bear. He threw himself into her sleeping arms and called to her, crying "Mother, Mother, why won't you wake up?"

Piffany waited until Bundla had stopped his crying and then gently nudged his fuzzy arm. "Why have your mother and all the other bears of your village fallen asleep in the courtyard?"

Bundla checked his sobs and said in a halting voice, "I don't know. They can't be hibernating for we always hibernate the day after Christmas. Not the day before. Not two days after."

He stopped for a moment and caught his breath as he wiped

an elusive tear from his eye with the corner of his mother's apron. "For you see, Piffany," he explained patiently, "the day after Christmas we un-decorate the Christmas tree. When all of us are ready for sleep and have our nightcaps on, one of us carefully removes the Morning Star from the top of the tree. When the star no longer rests on top of the tree and is safely stored away, all the bears of the village fall asleep wherever they are, which is usually in bed."

As Bundla spoke, he pointed a furry finger at the top of the tree and his eyes followed. Much to his surprise, the Morning Star of Christmas was gone!

Piffany followed his gaze. "But if the star is gone and all the other bears are asleep, why are you still awake?" she asked in her musical voice.

Bundla dropped his head in shame. "I am not asleep like the rest of my clan because I wasn't here when the star was removed." In a halting voice mixed with a sob here and there, the little bear told Piffany his story.

That very afternoon, just before twilight settled on the village of bears, Bundla had been asked by his mother to do a couple of chores. "But Mom!" he wailed. "Why do I have to?"

"Because," his mother answered patiently, "Christmas is a time of personal sacrifice and giving of one's self. You must learn to do this from the heart, Bundla, or you will never know true Christmas joy."

But instead of going to his room as he was told, Bundla ran outside and followed the cobblestone road deep into the forest.

"Sacrifice, shmackrifice! That's dumb!" Bundla muttered loudly and he kicked his sister, Honeybreath.

"That is enough from you, young bear!" his mother growled as she swatted him on the behind with a wooden spoon. "Now you just march up to your room and think about the meaning and true spirit of Christmas!"

But instead of going to his room as he was told, Bundla ran outside and followed the cobblestone road deep into the forest. He sat and pouted for hours and hours in an old rotted stump, waiting until he figured his mother was really worried about what had happened to him. When he thought it was time, he wandered back into the village.

That was when Bundla discovered that everyone, except himself, had fallen deeply asleep.

The little bear choked back a sob as he finished his story, "Someone must have stolen the Morning Star while I was hiding in the woods." With that, he broke into tears once again.

Piffany, moved by the little bear's distress, wrapped one of her large wings around his shoulders and comforted him as best she could.

They sat there in the courtyard for nearly an hour, consoling each other and staring blankly at the tree. Finally, Piffany roused from her reverie and said, "Bundla, who would steal the Morning Star? And why?"

Bundla thought for a moment. "I don't think it's a who, but rather a what, and I don't know why."

Not understanding, Piffany asked, "What did you say?"
"Yes," said Bundla solemnly.

"No, no," said a very confused Piffany. "I mean who?"
Bundla stared at her as if she were crazy. "I didn't say 'who', I said 'what'. You and I, we are 'who's'. The Dragon of Evilspell, she is a 'what'."

"And what, may I ask, is the Dragon of Evilspell?" Piffany asked with a chuckle.

"I will assure you that she is not a laughing matter," said Bundla solemnly. He proceeded to tell Piffany the legend of Crystal Mountain.

"Many, many years ago," the little bear began, "the bears of Kapriol were crude, lumbering beasts who shuffled and lumbered about the forest during the spring and summer. Late in the fall, they would burrow into the base of Crystal Mountain and sleep the cold winter away. One year an old

grey bear named Kursiff went searching for roots and berries to eat. He came upon the Morning Star which had fallen from the sky. When he and the other bears walked into its shining glory, they stood upright and began to think the most wonderful thoughts.''

"Winter ceased to be and there was only spring. All of the bears lived peacefully at the base of Crystal Mountain, slowly building this quaint, little village in its gentle shadow. There was food galore in the forest and because it was always spring, the bears never had to hibernate and sleep the winter away.''

"One day, as if from nowhere, dressed in a coat of ice scales and veiled in winter's mist, there swooped out of the sky a great and monstrous dragon named Evilspell. Her eyes were like frozen diamonds and her breath was like a crystal, blue flame that created a winter's chill. Evilspell told the bears of Kapriol that from that day forward, she would be their ruler and they would be her slaves. She commanded her new slaves to seek the two things that would allow her to rule the land forever: the Morning Star and the wings of a flying deer. With the wings she would create a royal cape and with the star, a scepter.''

"Kursiff, who had been elected mayor, roared loudly that she could never have the Morning Star. 'Leave our village forever!' he commanded. 'We will never be your slaves! And if you return,' he added, 'the village will eat Evilspell

"Leave our village forever!" he commanded.

stew, though it be tough and tasteless'."

"Evilspell grew livid, for she had never considered herself tasteless — maybe rude, maybe crude, but never tasteless."

"Not one to take defeat lightly, Evilspell stormed around the village, screaming and bellowing her frozen rage. Finally, she began to pick all the horrid little toadstool mushrooms that she could find. When she had picked a hundred or more, she breathed into them the breath of fire and ice, and all those ugly toadstools turned into grim-faced, squalid, horrid gnomes. Into a particularly misshapen mushroom, a little larger than the rest, she breathed more coldly than she had the others. With her wicked breath, the mushroom became the king of all the gnomes of Crystal Mountain, Vilespot," Bundla continued.

"When Evilspell was through with her mischief, she gathered her creations around her and commanded them to scour the land in search of the star and a winged deer. With Vilespot in the lead, the gnomes grinned their silly, lopsided smiles and trotted into the forest in search of their mistress's wishes."

"After days and days, they came cackling back through the trees like a fall storm gone bad, dragging with them a badly frightened flying deer. Vilespot, king of the gnomes, proudly presented their captive to Evilspell."

" 'But where, you rotten little toadstool, is the Morning Star? What good are the wings without the star?' she screamed in her iciest tone. 'The deer's wings without the star is like a banana split without the bananas!' She cuffed Vilespot so hard that he ended up standing on his head at the base of a tree. 'Now, listen again my little salad fixings. I need a winged deer and the Morning Star. Together, together, do you hear?' Dropping her voice to an icy whisper, she continued. 'Now listen carefully! When I have both of them, together, I will use the wings for my cape and the star will become my ruling scepter. But — they must be together! Now drag that flea-bitten animal to the caverns of Crystal Mountain. There she shall await her fate. I know where the star is and I will have it in the end!' "

"After the gnomes had gone, Evilspell began circling the village, blowing an icy wind and screaming vile curses, 'Give me the Morning Star, you walking, furry rugs, or I shall freeze the rain into crystal snow and the ice will come and never go!' But, the bears wisely held on to their star."

Bundla Joy stopped to catch his breath, then continued his story. "Evilspell, try though she might, could create only partial magic until she had the Morning Star. So from that day forward, three months out of every year she sat on Crystal Mountain blowing an icy wind that brought winter to

Kapriol causing the bears to hibernate the day after Christmas. Not a day before and not two days after. 'I can wait!' she'd cackle. And she was waiting still on the day I hid from my mother in the woods. That is, I thought she was,'' the little bear said with a last, hiccuping sob.

As Bundla finished his tale, Piffany was filled with horror. ''Did you say that Evilspell needed only the Morning Star and the wings of a flying deer to complete her magic spell and rule all of the land?''

''Yes,'' nodded Bundla sadly. ''The Morning Star for a scepter and the wings for a cape.''

Piffany's eyes were wide with fear, "Mother must have been captured by Evilspell and the gnomes," she cried. "Come! We must hurry!"

"Where are we going?" asked Bundla, who was afraid he knew the answer.

"To Crystal Mountain to get back your Morning Star and to rescue my mother!"

The two of them raced to Bundla's home on the square, where Piffany made sure the little bear put on a long woolen scarf, warm woolen mittens, and a knitted cap of eiderdown. Then, with the bear upon her back, Piffany lifted high into the skies of Kapriol.

She circled around and with each circle they climbed higher and higher. "Are you sure this is safe?" asked Bundla, holding on with all his might. But Piffany didn't answer, for her thoughts were lost on her mother and the gnomes of Crystal Mountain.

Slowly, like a monstrous sore on the face of the earth, the mountain began to loom above the forest. The higher they flew, the larger it seemed to become. Stronger and stronger Piffany beat her wings against the bitter cold of the night, and higher and higher they flew. As the oval moon hung in the sky with icy stars for a background, the two friends flew up and up until finally they were flying higher than the highest peak. Then and only then did the little deer slow her great wings to glide on the frozen winds.

Through teeth that chattered, partly from fear and partly from cold, Bundla asked, "What are we looking for, up here so high?"

Without relaxing her steady vigil, Piffany answered, "An entry into the mountain. The gnomes must have a way in and out of the mountain and the caverns. Look for a path that seems to end, going nowhere."

They searched throughout the night in the flat white light of the full moon. Then, just when they were about to give up in exhaustion, Bundla exclaimed, "There's an opening, a cave!" Sure enough, there on a ledge was the opening into the caverns of Crystal Mountain.

Mindful of her tail winds and careful not to be seen, Piffany landed quietly at the entrance. "This is it, all right!" she said in a whisper. "You can smell the evil on the wind."

Bundla stood on his tiptoes and scrunched his nose in disgust as he smelled the vileness and filth coming from the bowels of the mountain. "Well," he said nervously, "I guess we might as well go on in."

With that the two crept through the large, dark opening. The rocks reflected what light there was from the moonlight's glare and they could see clearly as they walked the winding trail. Step by step, they stealthily moved deeper and deeper into the mountain. It was so quiet, they could hear their own breath echoing in their ears.

Suddenly, out of nowhere, the air filled with black, flapping wings and high-pitched screeching. Bundla screamed as both he and Piffany leaped behind some rocks. There they crouched for a moment or two with wide eyes and thumping hearts. "What manner of evil was that?" the trembling bear asked.

Piffany looked about, then chuckled quietly. "Boy, we sure are brave. Look!" She pointed her wing at the ceiling of the cave entry where a very old bat hung upside down and looked at them through sleepy lids. "It was nothing, but a bat. Come on. We've got to find the gnomes' camp." She once again began walking down the path as it twisted between the cave's monstrous boulders.

Deeper and deeper into the cave they walked. The path turned dusty and began to slope down ever so gently. While, with every step they took, the moonlight faded in intensity, the cave seemed to get brighter — not with a clean, crisp light, but a dusty, orange and yellow glow that seemed to come from the very depths of the earth. The rocks were covered with fine soot, and the air was heavy with something very evil.

Bundla cleared his throat and said in a feathery whisper, "Are you sure we're in the right cave? Maybe we ought to go outside and check to make sure this is the right mountain."

"It's all right, Bundla," Piffany answered as she moved into the lead on the trail. "Remember what a wise man once said: 'You have nothing to fear but fear itself' ."

Bolstered by her confidence, the little bear quickened his pace to catch up and said, "Then I must be really scared, because I am really fearing fear itself."

Just as Piffany turned to answer, the world seemed to explode around her. Falling and jumping from the rocks above her were ugly, leather skinned gnomes. She felt them

Just as Piffany turned to answer, the world
seemed to explode around her.

surround her and then she was trapped; her whole body wrapped tightly in a coarsely woven net. "Get her, you slime buckets! Wrap her up. It seems we have another present for her highness, Evilspell." The cavern echoed with the gnomes' laughter as they roughly tied the poor winged deer into the net. But unnoticed throughout the excitement and all the fear, Bundla hid wedged between two sooty rocks.

As Piffany was dragged down into the cavern, he watched with large, frightened eyes. "What am I to do?" he whispered out loud. "I'm just too small to do any good. Besides, I've only known her for a few hours. I'm getting out of here!" With that he began to race back up the path. Bundla followed the twisting trail nearly all the way back to the entrance, but then fell to the ground with a racking sob.

"I can't! I just can't desert Piffany. I must go back," he murmured with deep resolve. "What was it that she said? 'You have nothing to fear but fear itself!' Yeah, that and a lebbity million gnomes and a dragon and a whole bunch of bats."

Bundla forced his feet to move, one after the other, as he retraced his tracks down, down into the caverns of Crystal Mountain.

With his heart thudding in fear and with a ringing in his ears, Bundla returned to the place where Piffany had been captured. In the dimly lit cavern, he could see where the gnomes had wrestled her to the ground. Step by painful step, he followed the trail deeper into the mountain. In the half-light, Bundla found himself walking into boulders or tripping over rocks with nearly every step. Each time, he slowly picked himself up and returned to the trail.

The light in the cavern became brighter and began to flicker and weave, allowing Bundla to see better than he wanted to see. Carefully, he flitted from shadow to shadow until he came to what appeared to be the very edge of the earth itself.

Then, crawling on all fuzzy fours, he inched his way to the edge of the precipice and looked down. There below him was the home of the Gnomes of Evilspell. Fires sputtered here and there, cooking this and warming that. Strange mushroom shaped tents made of odd-sized pieces of fur were scattered hither and thither. Squat, shadowy shapes scurried about the campsite shouting boisterously in the gutteral language of the gnomes.

Everywhere Bundla looked, there were gnomes. He lay his head in his furry paws and shook in a terrible fit of fear. He sobbed softly to himself for a moment or two and then realized it was time to do what had to be done. With a deep breath, he once again looked down into the cavern.

There, off to one side, near a pile of discarded furs, he spied a corral. Within it, tied to a post like a common horse, was Piffany. Steeled with resolve, Bundla slowly began to sneak down the path into the camp itself. The trail was littered with bits of bone and garbage discarded by the filthy gnomes. The evil smell of sulphur burped from cauldrons of glop cooking over the fires. The gnomes laughed and giggled at the smell like children catching their first delicious whiff of chocolate.

No matter how great his fear, Bundla forced himself to go on. Sneaking here and there, careful not to be spied, he finally stepped off the steep path and onto the floor of the cavern itself. The smells were much heavier there. Bundla quickly dashed behind one of the tents and leaned against a post to catch his breath.

It was only then that he realized the tent was made from the skin of some animal stretched over sticks and twigs. His eyes opened wide in horror as he realized that all of the tents were made from the skins of bears. He would have bolted right then and there and raced out to the cave if he had not heard a high, piercing scream followed by rales of coarse gnome laughter.

"That's Piffany's scream!" he said to himself. "And she's in trouble!" With that, Bundla quickly began slipping from one squat tent to another, moving toward the corral and the sound. Just as he raced around the corner of the final tent, he heard the scuffling feet of several gnomes right before him. Without thinking, he leaped into a pile of furs thrown carelessly nearby. He burrowed and burrowed until only his short, brown fluff of a tail peeked out.

Buried in his sanctuary with his paws covering his eyes, Bundla awaited his doom. The scuffling feet came closer and closer, finally stopping within inches of his hiding place. The gnomes spoke in muffled voices, but Bundla could hear every nasty word. "You! Slime bucket! Yeah, you! Grab me a fresh bear fur. I want to be dressed to kill when Evilspell crowns herself queen and supreme ruler of the land."

The poor little bear felt the dry, warted hands of a gnome pawing through the furs. He felt himself being lifted by his short, fluffy tail, but stayed just as still as could be as his unknowing captor held him high in the air. "Vilespot! How's this?"

"Wrong, mold mouth. That bit of moth-eaten fur wouldn't even make good shoes! Find another!"

With that, Bundla was thrown quite unceremoniously back into the pile. He was almost tempted to stand up and tell Vilespot that his fur was just as good as any other, but he realized that becoming a fine fur was a finality he didn't need to explore.

Rough boots kicked and booted him about as the gnome rooted through the furs, with Vilespot refusing one after another. "Hurry, worm breath! We must take the deer wing cape to Evilspell within the hour or she'll have our hides and we will be nothing better than toadstools again! There, that one will do just fine."

Their task complete, the two gnomes left the shaken bear alone in the pile of furs.

Bundla stood and looked around with tears streaming down his fur. "The scream I heard must have been Piffany as they turned her into a cape! Now she must be dead and all is lost!" His eyes blurred by tears, Bundla stumbled into the open. The gnomes were so caught up in their pre-celebration, they didn't even notice the sobbing bear as he wandered aimlessly about. Bundla staggered to the corral and, with his head cradled in his arms, began to sob loudly.

"Wrong, mold mouth. That bit of moth-eaten fur wouldn't even make good shoes! Find another!"

"Bundla!" a soft voice whispered. "Help me get free!"

"I can't help you now, Piffany, 'cause you're already dead," he sobbed.

"Not by a long shot, little bear!"

With that, Bundla lifted his head in wonder and there before him was Piffany, untouched and very much alive. "But I heard you scream and I thought..."

"It was I who screamed," said Piffany softly. "I couldn't help myself when the gnomes told me that they had taken the wings from my mother. But," she said with a deep sigh, "we have no time for sadness now. Untie me. For we must hurry to the cavern of Evilspell and find the Morning Star before all is lost for all the land."

As Bundla freed the winged deer, he told her what the gnomes had said at the pile of furs. "We must hurry," she said. "For there is no time to lose!"

With that, they carefully made their way to the steep path which would lead them out of the cave into the magical cavern of Evilspell.

Just as they began their journey up and away, Bundla spied the most beautiful cape he had ever seen. Left behind by the gnomes, the cape seemed to have been made with the gentleness of the morning mist and sewn together with shimmering spider webs that glistened with morning dew.

Trying to swallow the lump in his throat, Bundla asked, "Isn't that Evilspell's cape made from the wings of a flying deer?"

Piffany stopped to look. Diamond-shaped tears welled in her eyes as she saw the reminder of her mother. With grim resolve, she said, "My mother did not give up her wings in vain. Bundla, grab the cape and follow me; we will see how great this monster's magic can be!"

Bundla carefully gathered up the cape and together they began scurrying up the path. They climbed so high, that they could look down on the entire gross kingdom of the gnomes, far, far below.

As they watched, the deformed creatures below began to run around and around in mass confusion.

"Look!" said Piffany. "They've discovered the cape is missing!"

Sure enough, even at their great height, they could hear Vilespot screaming, "You dolts! You toad tongues! You've lost the cape. Now Evilspell will eat us like a candied treat."

As one, the gnomes looked up and began to point and shout in great agitation. "We've been spotted, Bundla!" shouted Piffany. "Now we must surely hurry or all will be lost." With that, they once again began their laborious climb. Higher and higher they climbed, with the gnomes climbing after them.

As the filthy gnome camp disappeared far below, the air became cleaner and much, much colder. Their breath formed a white, velvet fog as the two puffed higher and higher. The sandy path they had been running on began to crunch beneath their feet, and the rocks of the cavern glistened with frost and ice. Up and up they went with the gnomes cursing behind. Finally, as the trail turned sharply to the right, they slid to a stop in a great and monstrous cavern of natural ice that glittered like a thousand diamonds on a starlit night.

Bundla and Piffany had been running so hard that when they tried to stop they couldn't. They skittered and screeched across the icy floor, finally coming to rest in a heap at the base of a massive throne cast in frosty snow.

The two of them looked in total amazement at all there was to see. "Wow!" whispered Bundla in the echoing hall. "Where are we?"

Piffany carefully stood up as she answered, "This must be

the cavern of Evilspell!" Carefully she began to explore the massive room, which was bare save for the throne cast in a single piece of ice. "Bundla," she warned, "I think we had best find the Morning Star and then slip out of here!" The little bear just sat where he was, clutching the cape and staring about in dumb wonder.

Suddenly, the halls began to echo with the screams and vile curses of the gnomes. The two friends looked at one another and then, without talking, searched in vain for someplace to hide.

"Quickly," urged Piffany, "throw the cape beside the throne. We'll hide beneath it and pray they assume we've abandoned it."

Bundla tossed the cape to the side of the throne and they crawled beneath it. At the last moment, Piffany realized the little bears bottom was exposed for all to see, and just as the room exploded with gnomes, she grabbed his tail in her mouth and yanked the rest of him to safety.

The room rang and clashed with a cacophony of sound as the gnomes rushed here and there, looking for their prey. "Find them! Find them, you glopheads or we shall all be stew!" The hideous creations slipped and slid around the great room as Vilespot leaned on the throne. One of his floppy feet rested on the cape, which seemed to have been carelessly thrown on the floor.

His gaze greasily slid about the room and then, by

chance, he slowly looked down. "Ahh, ha!" he cackled as he beckoned to the other gnomes. "See, they were here. They've abandoned the cape." Just as he reached down to lift the cape, a blue ominous fog rolled along the frozen floor looking for something warm to hold. The walls started to rattle and bits of ice crumbled and crashed to the floor.

Vilespot forgot all about the cape, and he began to pace back and forth, back and forth. "Lordy, lordy, lordy! It's the queen of all the snowballs, the Dragon of Evilspell. We are sure to be tossed in the salad now. Lordy...lordy!"

The room seemed to ring with the tinkling of broken glass and shards of ice. It became colder and colder. Finally, when everyone's ears and noses seemed to be as cold as cold could be, the great frozen goddess of winter, the Dragon of Evilspell, slithered icily into the room. She stood nearly four snow shovels high at the shoulder, and her long neck went up from there. In one icy claw, she carried the Morning Star mounted on an ice pick. Rays of bright light reflected in her deep-black pupils and sent beams bouncing off the ceiling and walls. She gazed in mock wonder, taking in the scene before her.

"Well, well, well!" she said in a wintry tone. "Are we having a party?"

Vilespot moved quickly away from the throne, bowing and scraping. "No, your Arctic Majesty, we, uhh...That is, they kind of...well...you see..."

"Well, well, well!" she said in a wintery tone. "Are we having a party?"

"Enough of your blithering!" the ice queen bellowed in a blast of hoarfrost and rime. "You had best tell me what is going on here before I turn you all into ice scream gnomes!"

"We've, uhh," Vilespot began again, trying to make his feeble mind create a likely story. "We've come to bring you a present!" he continued as the cape caught his eye. "The great, magical cape made from the wings of a flying deer." With a flourish, he pointed his dirty, bent finger at the base of the throne. The cape seemed to shudder as if it were alive.

With all eyes riveted on the cape at the base of the throne, Evilspell began to slither her icy way across the floor. "Ahh! 'Tis done. All the magic in the world is now mine!" She glided up the steps and sprawled frozenly on the throne, waving the scepter idly in the air. "The first thing," she said in a chilling voice, "is to reverse the magic of Kapriol and turn those bumbling bears into the lumbering beasts they are supposed to be."

Bundla, still hidden beneath the cape, began to shiver uncontrollably. Piffany did all she could to keep him still.

"Before I waft the bears back to the berry patch, I'm going to cook that old, grizzled, mayor bear Kursiff and the young, delectable Honeybreath to make bear stew!" The cape shuddered once again as Bundla heard that even his sister was in mortal danger.

"But before I do anything," she said pointing an icicle finger at the leader of the gnomes, "I need to make you, Vilespot, my little frozen king."

"Who, uhh...me?" asked Vilespot stupidly, as he looked around desperately for someone to take his place. "I really don't want to be king. Maybe a prince or something, but not king."

Evilspell carefully laid the scepter of the Morning Star on the cape at the base of the throne and reached for the little misshapen creature before her. She was so intent on touching him that she didn't notice a soft, chubby paw reaching up

from beneath the cape. Five furry fingers wrapped themselves around the scepter and gently pulled it under cover.

If you had been listening very carefully, you would have heard hurried whispers. "Why did you do that? Now she'll find us for sure!"

"Yeah, but she was going to eat the mayor and my sister Honeybreath. Shh!"

Evilspell kept talking in her icy tone as she pulled Vilespot ever so near. "Now, my little popsicle, you shall be king!" With that, she reached down for the scepter and found it gone. "What!!" she howled. She leapt from the throne and looked at the cape as it began to move and shift.

"Well, my little friend, it's now or never!" said a resigned Piffany with a sigh. Together, she and Bundla stood with the cape draped over them, and like a ghostly form, began running from the hall.

The gnomes were frightened as the apparition of the living cape seemed to float by, and even Evilspell was taken aback, but only for a moment. "After them, you twits! They have the cape and the Morning Star!" She huffed and puffed, blasting an icy chill of glacier snow and frostbite ice.

The wind tore through the hall and nearly ripped the cape from Bundla's grasp as he clung to Piffany's back. With the scepter in one hand and the cape wrapped around his neck, Bundla hung on for dear life as the deer skidded and slid down the hall and out the frozen entry, with the gnomes in hot pursuit.

Down the path they raced, as rocks thrown by the vicious gnomes fell all around them. Through the corral, around the tents, with pots and pans flying in all directions, they raced for their lives and the lives of all the living creatures of Kapriol. Up the slimy path they ran, into the hallways that led out of Crystal Mountain. This time, when the bat flapped its wings, neither Piffany nor Bundla were startled in the slightest. Finally, in a puff of dust and pebbles, they skidded to a stop just at the edge of the caverns.

The still, starlit night blinked in welcome as Piffany spread her wings for flight. "I won't be afraid, Piffany," said Bundla. "Just fly us off this mountain!" Piffany flapped her wings slowly at first and then more quickly, but nothing happened. "Fly, Piffany, fly!" Bundla shouted through gritted teeth. He looked over his shoulder at the oncoming horde of gnomes.

"I can't!" Piffany cried. "The weight of you, the scepter, and the cape is too much for me to carry."

"Then you must leave me!" said Bundla, and he slipped from her back. "Take the Morning Star back to the village and hide it near the Christmas tree. Then, you can come back for me!"

Without a second thought for his own safety, and with the cape wrapped around him, Bundla rushed over the edge and down the steep path away from Crystal Mountain. The last the little bear saw of Piffany was her silhouette as she flew up and away. " At least she could have tried to talk me out of it!" he puffed, as his little legs pounded down the steep embankment and into the forests of Kapriol.

Far behind him (but not far enough), Bundla could see oily, smoking, flickering flames as the gnomes' torches reflected off the glittering scales of the Dragon of Evilspell. He could hear the shouts and pounding footsteps of his pursuers as they scrambled madly after him. His breath came in ragged gasps as he stumbled and ran and ran.

Mile after mile after mile, the poor little bear pushed on and on. Every short stride he took brought the dragon and her troops closer and closer. "No matter what happens," Bundla thought as he forced himself on, "Honeybreath and the rest of the bears are safe."

Suddenly, the forest became still and Bundla realized that he could no longer hear Evilspell screaming behind him. "Maybe, just maybe, I'm safe," he puffed as he rounded a corner of the trail. He stopped, put his hands on his knees and drew deep gulps of air into his lungs as he tried to catch his breath.

His reverie was broken by an icy, insidious voice, "Going somewhere, little bear?"

Bundla looked up. There, before him, stood Evilspell. He turned to dash back up the trail, but there were all the gnomes, with torches sputtering, mocking him with their vile smiles. "I think," said Evilspell in her coldest voice, "that

"At least she could have tried to talk me out of it!"

maybe I won't eat you as bear stew." Bundla breathed a sigh of relief. "No, I think I'd rather stuff an apple in your mouth and roast you like a pig in the oven!"

Slowly, the gnomes and Evilspell formed a sickly circle around the quaking bear, Bundla, who just stood there clutching the cape and looking oh, so frightened.

The slimy little gnomes and the icy Dragon of Evilspell circled around and around the frightened bear. With every turn they made, the circle grew tighter and tighter, until Bundla could smell their fetid breath. Step by agonizing step, they came closer and closer.

Without warning, a graceful form swooped down from the starlit sky and landed right before the crystal queen of doom. "What's the matter, dragon breath, cat got your tongue?" asked Piffany in a sing-song fashion.

Evilspell stood in furious, frozen anger and screamed, "Why you flea-bitten fur ball. I'll show you!" With that she breathed a monstrous blast of rime and frost. Just as she did so, Piffany lifted Bundla into the air and lit gently, two feet away. Instead of freezing her prey, Evilspell froze two gnomes right in their tracks.

"Temper, temper, snow lizard!" Piffany taunted.

Once again Evilspell let loose a mighty blast of bitter, biting snow, and once again Piffany leaped out of the way in the nick of time. Blast by icy blast, Evilspell froze everthing in sight. She froze the gnomes like ice cream cones, from

Vilespot down to the last ugly, little, misshapen monster. Finally, there were only three in the clearing in the wood: Evilspell, a tiring Piffany and one very amazed bear.

The dragon took another deep breath, but this time only pretended to blow. As before, Piffany lifted Bundla and moved him out of the way. Twice more the evil one feinted, and twice more Piffany fell for the ruse. At last, Piffany tired to the point that she couldn't fly anymore and with her head held low, she knew there was no escape.

Evilspell slowly turned and smiled her most wicked grin. "Now I can't miss! Can I?" With that, she took a mighty breath and exhaled as hard as she could at the cowering friends. But instead of a blast of cold air, she only coughed and burped a snowball. Like a hard winter's storm, Evilspell had blown herself out.

The dragon, with her tail swishing like an angry cat's, began to slink off into the woods. "I won't soon forget this, Piffany!" she warned. "I may not be able to beat you, but every year for two months, maybe three, I'll cast my spell and freeze the lakes and rivers so you'll never forget me. For someday, I vow to come back for the Morning Star and the cape of the winged deer!" With that, she slithered through the frozen mushroom gnomes and crawled back to her lair, high on Crystal Mountain. With utmost relief and joy at being saved from a frozen grave, Bundla rushed to Piffany and hugged her with all of his might. Finally, when all the tears of joy were dried, Piffany nudged her friend onto her back and flew away to the village of Kapriol.

Everything in the village was just as they had left it, save for the Morning Star, which Piffany had hidden at the base of the tree. "Bundla," she said, "you may have the honor of placing the star at the very top of the tree where all can see it. For today is Christmas day, not the day before and not the day after. All the bears should be awake and joyful."

Bundla carefully climbed the tree. With great ceremony, he placed the star exactly where it belonged. As if by magic, the tree seemed to light itself in wondrous splendor, and by its light all of the bears of Kapriol woke to a glorious Christmas morning.

Oh, how the bears asked questions and wondered at all that had transpired. Bundla, with Piffany's help, told his story from start to finish, ending with Evilspell's ominous winter warning. Even with the warning, the bears were delirious with joy at having such a special Christmas, when they might have all stayed asleep.

Their joy turned to sorrow as they watched Bundla pick up the crystal white cape and, with tears in his eyes, hand it to a very sad Piffany.

"I'm sorry about your mother, Piffany. I wish there was something I could do to bring her back," he said softly.

Piffany stared at the cape and replied, "Her memory will be with me always, but lest we forget that Evilspell needs the cape to do her vile magic...it must be destroyed!"

No bear wanted to destroy so gentle a memory of the winged deer, and they all pondered long and hard. Finally Piffany said, "In memory of my mother, I give to you the gift of the cape." With that, she soared high into the air with the cape gripped firmly in her mouth.

Round and round she flew, higher and higher until she was nothing more than a speck in the sky. Then, as if by magic, the cape dissolved into a hundred thousand snowflakes that fell like a beautiful mantle over the Christmas tree of Kapriol.

At that precise moment, out of the forest walked a beautiful deer. With a whoop and a giggle, Piffany swooped out of the sky and landed beside her. "Mother, mother!" she cried. "I thought you were dead."

"No, my little Piffany. It would take more magic than Evilspell has to kill a winged deer. When the gnomes took my wings, I couldn't fly, but I could surely run, and run I did."

"Come, then, mother. We must fly back to the herd and give them the joyous news."

"No, Piffany! I can never fly again, but must walk as mortal deer walk."

Only then did Piffany realize that her mother's wings were truly gone, and she began to cry small, frozen tears. All the bears gathered round, and gentle furred paws petted her sides in consolation.

"Not to worry," said Bundla. "Your mother can stay with us forever and a day, always to be cared for and loved by the bears of Kapriol."

Piffany's mother nuzzled her daughter and said, "You must go now, child. I will be happy here; I will watch as the bears do sleep for any signs of Evilspell. In the springtime, when the winds are sweet with blossoms, you can come back and visit as you wish."

Piffany kissed her mother gently on her velvet cheek, and with strong, powerful strokes lifted into the sky. With a swoop, she glided over the town and called out in her musical voice, "I'll go back to the herd now to tell them the news, but to all of you and for all of you...

MERRY, MERRY CHRISTMAS."

"...Merry, merry Christmas."